For Michael and Lucy

North American edition published 2021 by minedition US
A Division of Astra Publishing House, New York

Text and Illustrations copyright © 2021 by Dan Yaccarino
Coproduction with minedition Ltd., Hong Kong
Rights arranged with "minedition ag", Zurich, Switzerland. All rights reserved.
This book, or parts thereof, may not be reproduced in any form without permission
in writing from the publisher.
The scanning, uploading and distribution of this book via the Internet or via any other
means without the permission of the publisher is illegal and punishable by law.
Please purchase only authorized electronic editions, and do not participate in or encourage
electronic piracy of copyrighted materials. Your support of the author's rights is appreciated.
minedition US, 19 West 21st Street, #1201, New York, NY 10010
e-mail: info@minedition.com
This book was edited by Leonard Marcus and Maria Russo and printed in April 2021
at Grafiche AZ, Verona (BA), Italy
Typesetting in Longest Storm designed by Dan Yaccarino
Library of Congress Cataloging-in-Publication Data available upon request.

ISBN 978-1-6626-5047-5
10 9 8 7 6 5 4 3 2 1 First Impression

DAN YACCARINO

THE LONGEST STORM

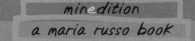

*min*edition
a maria russo book

A storm came to our town.
It was unlike any storm
we'd ever seen.

No one knew how long it would last. We were going to have to stay inside, maybe for a long while.

There was nothing to do,
and too much time to do it.

Being home together like that, all the time, felt strange.

But soon it went from strange

to bad,

to worse.

And just when it seemed like it couldn't get any worse...

We were completely sick of each other.

Is it possible for a family to run out of nice things to say?

Everyone just wanted to be alone.

At least that way we wouldn't get so mad all the time.

But then came the night we all

heard a rumbling in the distance.

There was a big flash.

The whole house shook.

Then nothing.

We all said we were sorry.

But not the storm.
It was still there.

Not having to stay inside together.
We still had to do that.

It was hard to say what had made the difference.

Someone would still get angry at someone else.

Just not for all that long.

Then things started to get better, a little every day.

Until things were good.

And then came one impossibly beautiful day
when the storm was gone.

We went outside.

There was so much to do.